The Thrift Store

TALES OF MYSTERY AND LORE

Kele Chi

All rights reserved.
© Kele Chi 2024

The right of Kele Chi to be identified as the author of this work has been asserted in accordance with the Copyright, Designs and Patents Act 1988.

This is a work of fiction. Names, characters, businesses, places, events, and incidents are either the product of the author's imagination or, if real, used fictitiously and therefore not necessarily factual or intended to be factual.

CONTENTS

Preface 5

Ballerina.. 9

The Portrait..47

Rebirth 74

The Girl Behind the Veil................................ 113

For anyone struggling, embrace who you are, seek help when needed, and remember that healing takes time, but you are never alone in the journey.

PREFACE

In the bustling metropolises of New York, London, New Orleans, and Paris, hidden amidst the labyrinth of streets and alleys, there exists a mysterious thrift store. No one can quite recall how they found it, nor are its doors ever seen by those who aren't meant to enter. For those who do stumble upon its shadowy threshold, the store appears to be an ordinary place filled with forgotten relics from lives long past. But for those carrying deep, unhealed wounds, this store offers something far more than trinkets and secondhand treasures.

The storekeeper, an enigmatic figure whose presence seems to transcend time and space, offers each visitor a mystical object that appears tailored to their unspoken pain. But as with all things steeped in dark magic, there is always a price. The objects carry a hidden curse – an offer of transformation that comes at the cost of confronting their greatest fears, regrets, and unresolved trauma.

In these pages, you will find four stories that follow troubled individuals whose lives are bound by this mystical store, though they live in different cities, their paths cross. In New York, a single mother and her disabled daughter struggle to survive. In London, an ageing aristocrat battles the onset of dementia and the loneliness of a forgotten life. In New Orleans, a washed-up rapper grapples with the wreckage of his shattered career. In Paris, a young woman haunted by a scarred past tries to find peace in a world that seems determined to reject her.

Each of these characters, despite living in far-flung corners of the world, is connected by their pain and the choices they make when confronted by the storekeeper's dark magic. Their stories echo across continents. Their journeys are intertwined by the powerful force of human suffering and the hope for redemption.

In this collection of short stories, you will follow these four individuals as they wrestle with their tragic pasts, unlocking the deepest corners of their souls. Each must decide whether to succumb to the darkness within or rise above the curse that threatens to consume them. For in the end, it is not the objects they carry that define them, but the choices they make when confronted with the truth of their pain.

Welcome to the world of the mysterious thrift store, where magic and tragedy intertwine, and where each soul must confront their demons—or be lost to them forever.

BALLERINA

New York City buzzed with its usual rhythm, a relentless hum of car horns, footsteps, and conversations floating up into the clear blue sky. But inside a small, worn dance studio nestled between two towering buildings, the sound was different. It was quieter, the scratch of ballet shoes against wooden floors and the soft counting of a woman who once danced on grand stages.

"One, two, three... reach, extend, hold... beautiful, girls, beautiful!" Ola's gentle yet firm voice echoes through the studio. The young dancers twirl and stretch, their faces lit up with concentration and effort. They look at her as if she were the sun, following her every word and every movement, as though she were their lifeline to the world of ballet. She watches their graceful movements and lightness on their feet, and a familiar ache settles in her chest. Once, she had danced like them—on bigger stages, in front of larger crowds. She had worn the costumes, heard the applause, and felt the thrill of being a prima ballerina. But that life felt like a lifetime ago, a distant echo.

"Alright, that's it for today," she says as she claps her hands softly.

The girls line up to curtsey to her, their bright faces glowing with excitement. "See you all tomorrow."

The girls chatter excitedly as they gather their things, filing out of the studio and into the busy city. Ola watches them leave, her smile fading as the door swings shut, leaving her alone in the dim studio. She leans against the barre, staring at her reflection in the mirror, the image of a woman who had once been so full of life, now tired and worn, her dark hair, rolled up into a messy bun, her eyes carrying the weight of the years.

She slowly turns her gaze to the back corner of the studio, where her daughter sits quietly in a small wheelchair. Ada, her beautiful, delicate daughter with soft brown curls and bright hazel eyes, had been born with legs that would never support her and would never carry her across a stage like Ola once had.

Ola walks over and kneels beside her. "How's my little girl doing?" she asks softly, tucking a stray curl behind Ada's ear.

Ada looks up and smiles, her eyes filled with that pure, unfiltered joy that only children seem to have. "They were so good today, Mom. I liked how they did the pirouettes. Are you going to dance again?"

The innocent and sweet question always stirs deep emotion in Ola. Ada asks it often, and it hurts the same each time. Ola hesitates before answering, trying to keep her voice steady.

"I'm teaching now, honey," she says, gently stroking Ada's hand. "That's enough for me."

Ada tilts her head, unconvinced. "But you used to be the best, right? You could still be."

Ola smiles, her throat tightening. "You're sweet, baby. But things are different now."

Different. That's what she always said, but "different" was a placeholder for so many emotions she couldn't quite articulate.

After Ada was born, Ola had taken a break from ballet, thinking she'd return once her daughter was old enough. But when the doctors confirmed Ada's condition, that she would never walk, let alone dance, Ola knew her life had changed forever. She couldn't be a ballerina and be the mother Ada needed. So, she had left the stage behind—no more performances, rehearsals, or applause. She was choosing, instead, to teach ballet in a tiny studio that barely covers the bills, fighting to make ends meet in a city that moves faster than she can keep up with.

"Come on, let's get you home," Ola says, standing up and moving behind Ada's wheelchair. She wheels her to the door, the familiar creak of the old building echoing as they leave.

The streets of New York feel colder as they step outside. The late afternoon sun is beginning to dip behind the skyscrapers, casting long shadows across the sidewalks. Ola strolls, one hand on Ada's wheelchair, the other clutching a plastic bag containing a few groceries she had managed to pick up earlier. A road diversion causes them to take an unfamiliar route, where they come across a thrift store. Something catches Ada's attention, and she beckons her mum to stop. She peers through the shop window, her nose pressed against the glass, eyes wide and brimming with excitement. She eagerly points at a pair of worn pink pointe shoes hanging from a hook.

"That! That! That!" Ada screams, her small hand shaking as she points. "I want that!" she yells at her mother, her voice breaking with a desperation born from childhood dreams.

Seeing what Ada is so excited about, Ola takes a slow breath, her heart sinking. The dusty, second-hand pointe shoes still gleam in the light as if imbued with the hopes of every ballerina who ever wore them. She fights back tears, her chest tightening as she ponders Ada's fascination with ballerinas, a dream that grows fiercer every year.

"Please, Mum," Ada pleads, her hands clasped together as she looks up at her mother. "Please, can I have those?"

"Of course, sweety," Ola replies, forcing a smile, her voice warm but heavy with a kind of sadness Ada cannot understand. She steps behind her daughter's wheelchair, her hands tightening on the worn leather handles, and pushes her forward into the shop, the old door creaking as it swings open.

Inside, the store smells of dust, mothballs, and a hint of frankincense. It is a cramped, cluttered place filled with forgotten items from lives long past. The shelves are crowded with forgotten trinkets, tattered books, and mismatched furniture, all piled together in a chaotic display of old and unwanted things. It's the kind of place you might pass by without a second glance unless, like them, you are drawn by something special through its doors.

Ola swallows hard as they approach the counter, her eyes lingering on the price tags scattered across the items. Most were beyond what she could afford, but Ada's happiness mattered more than her financial worries.

The shopkeeper, an older woman with a face that seems to be carved from stone, watches them intently from behind the counter. Her silver hair cascades down her back and shoulders, and she wears a deep green shawl that drapes over her thin shoulders like an ancient relic. Though clouded with age, her wrinkled eyes gleam excitedly as Ada's wheelchair creaks across the uneven wooden floor.

"Those shoes," Ola begins, her voice trembling as she gestures toward the display in the window. "How much are they?"

The storekeeper shifts her gaze from Ola to Ada, her expression softening as she notices Ada's eager eyes fixed on the pointe shoes.

"The shoes, hmm?" the shopkeeper mutters, moving from behind the counter, her movements strangely graceful for someone her age. She walks over to the window display, her gnarled fingers brushing lightly against the worn satin shoes as though they held some kind of delicate magic. She lifts them from the hook, turning them over in her hands before returning to the counter.

"They've been here for quite some time. I'm surprised anyone's taken notice of them," she says softly as if speaking to herself.

Ola bites her lip, her eyes darting to the old shoes. They were frayed at the edges, the satin dulled and scuffed, but to her daughter, they were priceless. She could see how her little girl's eyes sparkled, as though nothing else mattered more at that moment.

"How much?" Ola asks again, her voice more insistent this time.

The shopkeeper's lips curled into a slow, enigmatic smile that didn't quite reach her eyes. "Oh, I'm sure we can make an arrangement," she says, almost cryptic. "But... why the shoes?"

Ada, who had been silent until now, speaks up. Her voice is soft but filled with determination. "Because I want to be a ballerina," she says, her tiny fingers clutching the edge of her wheelchair. "I want to dance like my mum."

The shopkeeper looks taken aback momentarily, her ancient eyes glinting with something unreadable. She leans closer to the child, her voice barely a whisper. "And you think these shoes will help you dance?"

Ada nods, her eyes bright with hope. The shopkeeper chuckles softly, sounding like the rustling of old leaves. "These shoes have danced many times before. They belong to someone else's story. But perhaps..." She trails off, her gaze wandering to a small shelf behind the counter. There, sitting beneath a glass dome, is a delicate music box. The figurine inside is a ballerina, spinning gracefully in mid-leap, frozen in time. It is small but intricately carved, its wooden base polished to a soft sheen. "Perhaps you'd like this instead?"

Ola squints, taken aback. "But she doesn't want a music box. She wants the shoes."

The shopkeeper's smile widens. "The shoes come with their own history, but this," she said, nodding toward the music box, "holds a different kind of magic. I think you'll find it more suited to your daughter."

"Really! "What does it do?" Ada bursts with excitement.

The shopkeeper's smile deepens, her voice dropping to a hush. "It can take you to places you've never imagined. Places where your dreams come true."

"Thank you, but we don't believe in magic," Ola exclaims.

Ada stares at the music box, transfixed by the ballerina inside. Her heart races as the figurine seems to beckon her, inviting her into a world she longed to be a part of.

"Mum," she whispers. "Can I have the music box too? Please?"

Ola sighs, glancing at the shopkeeper with uncertainty. "I'm not sure we can afford both," her voice quiet, almost apologetic.

The shopkeeper's gaze shifts back to Ola, and there's something cold in her eyes for a moment. But then the smile returns, broader now, quite animated. "For you, a special offer," she says. "The shoes and the music box—two for the price of one."

"Mum, please," Ada whispers, her voice trembling with excitement. "Can I have both?"

Ola hesitates, staring at the shoes and the music box, feeling a strange chill settle over her. There was something unusual about the storekeeper's voice, something in the air that felt different, like a shift in the wind. But she can't bear to say no when she looks down and sees her daughter's eyes filled with such desperate hope.

"All right," she says softly. "We'll take them both."

The shopkeeper's eyes gleam with satisfaction as she carefully places the shoes and the music box into an old, worn bag. "Take care of them," she says, her voice low, almost warning. "They have a way of revealing things."

Ola frowns but nods politely, handing over what little money she has. As they leave the shop, Ada cradles the bag in her lap, her eyes still fixed on the music box inside. She can already feel the soft pull of its magic, the way it seems to call to her in a voice only she can hear. Ola fights back tears as she ponders her daughter's impossible dream. The wheelchair didn't stop her from dreaming of dancing on stage, light as air, like the ballerinas she so admired.

Lost in thought, Ola grazes shoulders with an elderly gentleman entering the shop as they leave. She apologises profusely, placing her hand lightly on his upper arm. He shrugs, gives her a condescending look and walks away without uttering a word.

That night, after they return to their small, dimly lit apartment on the third floor of a rundown building in Queens, Ada sits in her room, the pointe shoes lying next to her on the bed, the music box cradled in her lap, her hands trembling as she carefully opens the lid. A lullaby's soft, tinkling notes fill the room, and the tiny ballerina inside begins to spin, her delicate limbs frozen in a perfect arabesque. The way the ballerina twirled felt... alive.

As the music plays, Ola stands in the doorway, watching Ada with a tender but worried expression. The sight makes her heart ache. Ada loves ballet as much as she does, maybe even more. But Ada would never dance—not the way Ola had. Ola had given up her dreams for Ada and would do it a thousand times without hesitation. But still, the ache remained, deep in her bones, in her muscles that still remembered what it was like to soar across a stage.

With a heavy sigh, she says, "Don't stay up too late, okay? It's been a long day."

"I won't," Ada replies, her voice distant as she traces her fingers over the wooden base of the music box. "Goodnight, Mum."

"Goodnight, sweety," Ola says softly before returning to the kitchen, where the weight of their day seemed to press down on her shoulders.

Alone in her room, Ada lifts the shoes, running her fingers over the satin. They are worn, the edges frayed, but to her, they are the most beautiful thing in the world.

She carefully slips them onto her limp feet, though they are slightly oversized. She looks in the mirror, imagining herself standing on a grand stage, twirling and leaping like the dancers in her favourite movies. Then, her eyes fall on the music box again. Her heart races with anticipation as she winds the key on the side, the soft clicks of the mechanism filling the quiet room. The music begins to play—a soft, haunting melody that makes the hairs on her arms stand on end. The ballerina inside the box starts to spin, twirling gracefully to the rhythm of the music. Ada watches, transfixed, as the world around her seems to blur and fade.

A strange warmth spreads through her legs and a sensation she had never felt surges through her. Slowly, hesitantly, she tries to move her toes inside the pointe shoes—and to her shock, they respond. She gasps, her heart pounding in her chest. She moves her legs again, and this time, they obey.

She stands up, unaided. Ada looks down at her feet, disbelief flooding her mind. The pointe shoes feel weightless as if they lift and guide her. She takes a tentative step forward and then another. It is as if she has never used a wheelchair. Tears fill her eyes as she twirls around the small room, her heart soaring joyfully. The music from the box swells, growing louder and more enchanting. The world around her shimmers, and suddenly, everything goes dark.

When she opens her eyes again, she stands in the middle of a vast, beautiful ballroom. The floor beneath her feet is made of marble, and towering chandeliers sparkle from above, casting a warm, golden glow over the room. She is no longer in her small, cramped apartment. She isn't in her room. This is somewhere else—somewhere magical. The marble floor beneath her sparkled like a mirror, reflecting the thousands of tiny lights that twinkled above like stars captured in crystal chandeliers. She is dressed in a magnificent ballet costume—layers of delicate tulle in shades of pink and gold that float around her like a soft cloud. Her hair is swept up into an elegant bun adorned with glittering jewels that catch the light every time she moves. The rich scent of roses and vanilla fills the air. The silence is thick, almost expectant, as if the air around her held its breath.

"Hello?" she calls out, her voice echoing in the empty hall.

A soft, melodic voice answers her. "Welcome, Ada."

Ada spins around to see a woman standing at the far end of the ballroom. The woman is tall and elegant, dressed in a flowing gown that shimmers like starlight. Her dark hair cascades down her back in soft waves, and her eyes gleam with an otherworldly light.

"Who are you?" Ada asks, "And how do you know my name?" Her voice trembling with awe.

The woman smiles, her red lips curling into a beautiful, unsettling smile. "I am the Queen of Dreams," she responds, her voice as smooth as silk. "And you, my dear, have pranced your way into my realm."

Ada's heart races with excitement and wonder. "Is all this... real?"

The Queen nods slowly. "It is as real as your dreams, little one. Here, you can have everything you've ever wanted. You can dance, walk, run—anything your heart desires."

Ada's eyes widened with disbelief. "I can dance?"

"Yes," the Queen says softly, her voice soothing and hypnotic. "And you can stay here, where your dreams become reality."

Ada looks down at her feet, still wearing the pointe shoes. She can feel their magic humming through her legs, the power to walk and dance coursing through her veins. It is everything she had ever wanted.

Suddenly, orchestral music fills the air. The sound of violins swells, rising in a graceful, soaring melody. Ada gasps as an entire orchestra materialises around her, musicians dressed in formal attire, their instruments gleaming, shimmering into existence as if conjured by the music itself. The soft hum of cellos joins the violins, followed by the rich piano tone and the harp's delicate pluck. Each note wraps around her, lifting her soul and beckoning her to move.

The ballroom begins to transform. The ornate walls stretch and shift, moulding themselves into new shapes. Velvet drapes in deep crimson unfurl from the ceiling, cascading down the sides of the room. Golden lights beam down from above, illuminating the space around her, making her feel like she is standing in the very centre of the universe. The floor beneath her gently lifts, becoming a grand stage polished to perfection. Massive red curtains, rich and heavy, pull away with a dramatic flourish, revealing an audience that stretches beyond the horizon—faces glowing with anticipation, eyes fixed solely on her. She is the star.

The lights dim around the audience, focusing intensely on her. She is bathed in a soft spotlight that seems to illuminate her very soul. The music pauses for a heartbeat, and she feels the audience hold their breath in that silence. The orchestra's music swells, filling the grand hall with a melody that feels like it was composed just for her. She begins to dance.

Her feet glide effortlessly across the stage. The pointe shoes carry her in perfect pirouettes, her arms rising gracefully above her head as she twirls. Her movements are a seamless blend of strength and elegance. The music flows through her, every note translating into motion as if she and the orchestra are one. Time seems to slow down; each second stretches into eternity as she loses herself in the dance. For the first time in her life, she wasn't just watching ballerinas— she was one.

She executes a flawless grand jeté, soaring through the air as light as a feather before landing softly on the tips of her toes. The audience gasps in awe, the sound echoing like a gentle wave. She spins across the stage, her tutu fluttering like the wings of a delicate butterfly. Her arms move with the fluidity of water, and her expression is one of pure joy—a smile that radiates warmth and lights up her entire face.

As the final notes of the music swell to a crescendo, she strikes her last pose—a perfect en pointe, one leg extended behind her, arms gracefully arched above her head. The spotlight intensifies for a moment before slowly fading, leaving her bathed in a soft glow.

For a moment, there is complete silence. Then, as if the world had suddenly come back to life, the audience erupts into thunderous applause. The sound is overwhelming—a roaring ocean of cheers and clapping fills the air. People rise from their seats in a standing ovation, their faces alight with admiration and gratitude. Bouquets of vibrant flowers begin to rain down upon the stage—roses, lilies, orchids—all landing gently at her feet.

She stands there, breathing hard but feeling more alive than ever. Her heart swells as she looks out over the sea of smiling faces, each a testament to her performance. The admiration washing over her is like nothing she has ever experienced. It is intoxicating and exhilarating—a dream come true in every sense.

Tears of joy well up in her eyes as she bends down with trembling hands to pick up a single rose, its petals as red as the curtains that framed the stage. She holds it close to her heart, closing her eyes momentarily to savour the overwhelming happiness that fills her. She can see tears on some faces and smiles on others. They are here for her, celebrating her.

At this moment, she feels complete. All the struggles and pain of her real life have faded away. Here, she was not just a girl who dreamed of dancing—she was a prima ballerina, celebrated and loved. The dream realm had given her everything she had ever wished for, and she basked in its glow. This was where she belonged.

Ada catches sight of the Queen of Dreams standing off to the side of the stage. The

Queen's eyes glitter with satisfaction, and her smile is wide and inviting. She raises a delicate hand and gestures for Ada to come to her.

"Did you see them?" Ada exclaims as she reaches the Queen. "They loved it! They loved me!"

"Of course they did, my dear," the Queen purrs, her voice as smooth as silk. "This is where you belong. Here, you can dance forever and be adored by all."

Ada turns back to gaze at the audience once more. They were still clapping, their faces filled with joy and admiration. It was a sight she wanted to hold onto forever.

"I've never felt like this," she whispers. "It's everything I've ever wanted."

The Queen places a gentle hand on her shoulder. "And it can always be this way.

Stay with me, and every night will be just like this one—or even grander."

The idea was tempting, almost irresistible. Ada feels a pull in her heart, a longing to remain in this perfect moment. The world beyond the dream seemed so far away, so dim in comparison to the brilliance of the stage and the warmth of the audience's love.

But then, amidst the thunderous applause, a faint sound reaches her ears—a familiar voice calling out to her.

"Sweetheart..."

Her mother's soft, filled-with-love voice cuts through the noise and grounds her momentarily.

She looks up at the Queen, confusion flickering in her eyes. "I... I think my mum is calling me."

The Queen's smile tightens ever so slightly. "It's just the echoes of your old life, my dear. Here, you have all you need. The adoration of thousands, the freedom to dance, walk, and be whoever you wish."

Ada hesitates, her gaze drifting between the radiant audience and the shadowy edges of the stage where the Queen is standing. The allure of the dream was strong, but the faint call of her mother tugged at her heart.

"Can I show my mum?" she asks, hoping. "Can she be here with me?"

The Queen's eyes flash with something cold. "I'm afraid that's impossible," she says, her tone gentle but firm. "This realm is for you alone. It is the price you must pay to live your dreams."

A sense of unease begins to creep into Ada's joy. "But I miss her," she says softly. "I want her to see me dance."

The Queen's grip on her shoulder tightens almost imperceptibly. "In time, you'll forget about that world, and your mum will forget about you. The pain of separation is the sacrifice you must make."

The applause begins to fade, and the audience grows silent. The faces that had been so animated a moment before seem distant, their features blurred.

Ada looks back at the sea of people, confusion and doubt clouding her mind. "Why are they disappearing?"

The Queen's smile disappears. "You must make a choice, my dear. Leave your old world of misery behind and embrace this new life of dreams."

The stage lights dim, and the grandeur of the ballroom starts to waver as if it were a mirage dissolving in the heat.

Panic wells up inside Ada. "I don't understand."

The Queen leans in closer, her eyes piercing. "All you need to understand is that you can have eternal joy here. No pain, no limitations. Just endless admiration and the freedom to dance."

Ada steps back, pulling away from the Queen's touch. "But it's not real, is it? None of this is real."

The Queen's expression hardens, and a hint of frustration seeps through her composed facade. "What does it matter if it's real? Happiness is all that counts. Make your choice now!"

Tears begin to form in Ada's eyes. "I want my mum. I want to go home."

The Queen's eyes flash with anger. "You cannot leave now. The choice has been made."

Fear grips Ada's heart. "No! I want to go back!"

Her mother's voice comes through again, "Ada, take off the shoes."

She glances down at her feet and remembers the pointe shoes—they are the key. With trembling hands, she reaches down to untie them.

"Stop!" the Queen commands, her voice echoing ominously throughout the emptying hall.

But Ada doesn't listen. She pulls off the shoes, and as soon as they leave her feet, the world around her begins to crumble. The grand stage, the chandeliers, the velvet curtains all fade into darkness.

The Queen's form distorts, and her beauty twists into a sneer of fury. "You cannot escape me!" she hisses, reaching out with clawed hands.

Ada closes her eyes tight, clutching the pointe shoes to her chest. "I want to go home! I want my mum!" she cries out.

A sudden jolt and everything goes silent.

Ada wakes up with a gasp, her heart pounding in her chest. She is back in her bedroom, the soft morning light filtering through the curtains. The music box sits quietly on her bedside table, the ballerina inside motionless. The pointe shoes are on the bed beside her.

Her mother sits at the edge of her bed, concern etched into her gentle features. "Are you alright, sweetheart? You were crying in your sleep."

Ada throws her arms around her mother, holding her tightly. "Oh, Mum! I had the strangest dream."

Ola hugs her back, stroking her hair soothingly. "It's okay. I'm here."

Ada pulls back slightly to look into her mother's eyes. "I danced, Mum. I really danced. It felt so real."

A sad smile comes on Ola's lips. "I know how much you wish you could dance."

Ada shakes her head. "No, it was amazing, but... it wasn't worth losing you."

Ola's eyes glisten with tears. "You could never lose me, darling."

They sat there for a moment, wrapped in each other's arms. Ada feels a warmth and peace that no dream could ever replace.

Ada didn't know that her mum also had a strange dream. It was so bizarre and terrifying that she stayed up all night praying.

Ada glances over at the music box and the pointe shoes. A shiver runs down her spine as she remembers the Queen's sinister smile.

"Maybe we should get rid of those," she whispers.

Ola follows her gaze. "I think we should."

Ada nods. "Yes. I think it's time to let them go."

Ola squeezes her hand. "Alright. We'll take them back to the shop today."

Relief washes over her. "Thank you, Mum."

As they prepare for the day, Ada feels a newfound appreciation for the world around her—the soft texture of her blanket, the smell of breakfast wafting from the kitchen, and the simple joy of her mother's presence. At that moment, she knew she had made the right choice. Dreams could be beautiful, but the love of her mother was the most magical thing of all.

After dropping Ada off at school, Ola heads to the studio for her morning class. It's empty when she arrives. The light filtering through the large windows casts long shadows on the wooden floor. She has an hour before her first class, and for some reason, maybe because of the emotions that had bubbled up the night before, she feels a strange urge she hasn't felt in years. She stands in the centre of the room, looking at her reflection in the mirror. Slowly, hesitantly, she moves into first position, her feet instinctively finding the proper placement. She shuts her eyes and takes a deep breath.

And then, for the first time in years, she begins to dance. At first, her movements are tentative and rusty. But as she continues, muscle memory kicks in, and the grace she had once possessed comes flooding back. Her body remembers what her mind had forgotten—the joy, the freedom, the pure love of movement. She twirls and leaps, the wooden floor creaking under her feet, the quiet studio filling with the sound of her breath and the soft scuff of her shoes.

She was back on stage momentarily, the lights blinding, the audience watching in awe. For a moment, she was weightless again.

When she finally stops, she is out of breath, her chest heaving, but she feels alive in a way she hasn't in years. She looks at her reflection, her face flushed, her eyes bright, and she smiles—really smiles.

Ola knows she will never be a professional dancer again. That part of her life was over; she had made peace with it long ago. But dancing didn't have to be about performing or applause. It could just be for her. And for Ada.

She would teach her daughter everything she knows about ballet—the joy, the discipline, the beauty. Ada might never dance like she had, but that doesn't matter.

What matters is that Ada feels the magic of it the way she has.

Ola glances at the clock. It is almost time for her first class. She takes one last deep breath, brushes a stray lock of hair out of her face, and walks to the door, ready to face the day.

As she opens the door to let her students in, the ache in her chest is still there, but it is different now. It isn't the ache of loss anymore. It is the ache of love—a love that dances through every part of her, even if no one else can see it.

On her way to pick Ada up from school that afternoon, she passes by the thrift store to drop off the pointe shoes and music box. When she gets to the thrift store, it is empty and abandoned, covered in dust and cobwebs, as if no one has been there in years. Ola leaves the pointe shoes and music box on the floor in the centre of the store and walks away.

THE PORTRAIT

The rain fell softly over London, a grey drizzle that blurred the city's sharp edges, turning the world outside into a muted canvas. Lord Bartholomew Goodfellow sat in a high-backed chair in his grand manor in Kensington, gazing out at the foggy garden beyond the window, though his mind wandered far from the present.

The manor, a towering testament to his fortune, stood like a relic from a forgotten era. Its grand chandeliers, antique furniture, and halls adorned with portraits of his ancestors, told stories of generational wealth, privilege, and aristocracy. Yet the halls were silent now, except for the faint ticking of an old grandfather clock in the corner. At eighty, Lord Bart, as he preferred to be addressed, had outlived his family, friends, and even his own mind.

In his youth, Lord Bart was arrogant, entitled, and impossibly detached from the world's everyday struggles. He had never worked a day—his fortune, passed down through generations of Goodfellows, had ensured that. He was cynical and classist, never understanding or caring to understand the lives of those beneath him. For decades, he had cultivated an image of himself as a man above all others, apart from the rabble of London's streets.

Yet now, in the twilight of his life, dementia had begun to creep into his mind. It was subtle at first—a misplaced object, a forgotten name. But over time, it had grown more insidious. His once-sharp wit dulled, his thoughts muddled by a disease he could not control. Still, he tried to maintain his pride, even as reality slipped through his fingers.

His only companion in these darkening days was George, his butler of over forty years. As Lord Bart aged and dementia began to creep in, George's role shifted from butler to full-time caregiver. This was a responsibility that George took on without complaint, though it was far more demanding than his original duties. He monitored Lord Bart's medications, helped him dress, and reminded him of simple things, like the day of the week or the names of people long forgotten. George had served Lord Bart with the kind of loyalty one might mistake for friendship, though Lord Bart had never indeed seen it that way. To him, George was a fixture of the manor—

necessary, efficient, and, above all, obedient. Over time, however, even Lord Bart could not deny that George had become something more than just a servant. Perhaps he was the only person Lord Bart had ever truly cared about, though he would never admit it aloud.

One afternoon, Lord Bart had wandered out of the house while George was in the kitchen preparing his tea. By the time George realised, the old man had already made it halfway down the street, still in his dressing gown, muttering incoherently about catching the evening train to Oxford—a train that hadn't existed in years. It took George an hour to coax him back home, during which Lord Bart had called him "Thompson" several times, mistaking him for a servant long dead.

Another time, Lord Bart had grown convinced that his father, who had passed away when he was a boy, was visiting the manor. He had set the table for two in the grand dining room and ordered George to prepare his father's favourite brandy. George had complied, knowing better than to argue, but the episode ended with Lord Bart standing in the empty room, tears in his eyes as he called out to a man who had been gone for decades.

When Lord Bart had his episodes of confusion, wandering through the house and calling out to people who weren't there, George gently redirected him. On more than one occasion, George had found Lord Bart wandering outside in his dressing gown, convinced he was on his way to some long-forgotten party. George would bring him back inside each time, never once expressing frustration or impatience.

The toll of caring for someone with dementia was immense, but George bore it with quiet dignity. He never sought recognition nor resent Lord Bart for the increasing demands on his time. In his mind, this was just another duty, albeit one that required more of his emotional reserves than he'd anticipated.

Each incident seemed to chip away at what little was left of Lord Bart's mind, leaving George to pick up the pieces. The butler had grown accustomed to these lapses, but they seemed to hurt more each time. Once so proud and powerful, Lord Bart was now adrift in a sea of confusion, and George could only watch as the man he had served for so many years slowly faded away.

One dreary afternoon, Lord Bart and George drove through London in the Rolls Royce, heading toward an antique dealer in Knightsbridge. Lord Bart had always been an avid collector of antiques, a passion that had sustained him long after his other interests had waned. The car rolled to a slow stop at a red light, and Lord Bart gazed out of the window, his eyes catching on a small, shabby-looking shop across the street. Its sign was faded, and the windows were cluttered with odds and ends, but something about it called to him.

"Stop the car, George," Lord Bart said, his voice sharp with sudden clarity.

"Sir? We're not at the destination—"

"I said stop the car!"

George obediently pulled over, though his brow furrowed with concern. Lord Bart rarely gave commands with such force anymore. As the car stopped, Lord Bart peered through the rain-spattered window at the shop. Something about it stirred a memory deep within him—though he couldn't quite place what it was.

"I'll be just a moment," Lord Bart said, unbuckling his seatbelt.

"Allow me to accompany you, sir," George said gently, already moving to open his door.

"Nonsense, George. Stay here. I'll be fine on my own," Lord Bart snapped, his old arrogance flaring up. "I am not a child."

George hesitated but nodded. "As you wish, sir."

Lord Bart stepped out of the car, the cool rain brushing his face as he crossed the street. The shop loomed before him, small and unassuming, but there was something about it—something that pulled at him like a string tied to his past.

As he reached the entrance, a woman in a long coat was leaving, pushing a wheelchair with a child. The woman apologised as they grazed shoulders, but Lord Bart ignored her. His disdain was palpable as he gave her a condescending glance before brushing past them into the shop.

The air inside was thick with dust and the scent of old leather. The shop was cluttered with all manner of objects—antique clocks, silver candlesticks, and forgotten trinkets. But none of it interested Lord Bart. He wandered through the narrow aisles, his eyes scanning the shelves for something—he wasn't sure what.

The shopkeeper, a tall woman with unnervingly pale skin and eyes that seemed too dark for her face, greeted him from behind the counter. "Good afternoon, sir. Are you looking for something special?"

Lord Bart ignored her, his eyes continuing to sweep the room. After several minutes of fruitless searching, he sighed and turned toward the door, ready to leave.

But then, something caught his eye.

In the far corner of the shop, half-hidden beneath a pile of old books was a picture frame. It was simple, with a tarnished silver edge, but inside the frame was a portrait of a young woman. She was beautiful—her dark hair swept back, her eyes soft and kind. She looked familiar—too familiar.

Lord Bart's breath caught in his throat. He stepped closer, his hands trembling as he reached for the frame. The woman in the picture... it couldn't be. But it was.

It was her. "Agatha..." he whispered, his voice barely audible.

Agatha had been the light of Lord Bart's life, a bright, shining contrast to the dark corridors of wealth and privilege he had been raised in. They had met in the most unremarkable circumstances—at a ball hosted by one of his many aristocratic acquaintances—but something in him shifted from the moment he saw her. She wasn't like the other women in his social circle, who were polished, perfectly poised, and carefully bred to fit the narrow mould of high society. No, Agatha was different.

Born into a modest family, Agatha was introduced to London society by a distant cousin who had married into wealth. She had no grand inheritance, no sprawling estate to call her own. Yet, she carried herself with a grace and intelligence that captured Lord Bart's attention immediately. She had a fire in her eyes, a passion for life that he had never seen in anyone else. While he had spent his life shielded from the world's hardships, she had lived them, yet she was unburdened by the bitterness that often accompanied those struggles. She was real—alive in a way Lord Bart had never been.

Their courtship was swift but intense. Accustomed to getting whatever he wanted, Lord Bart relentlessly pursued Agatha, but she didn't make it easy. She was sharp-tongued and clever, constantly challenging his preconceptions about the world. She questioned his entitlement, his privilege, and, most daring of all, his outlook on life. Where Lord Bart saw the world through a lens of superiority, Agatha saw beauty in its imperfection. She had no illusions about his wealth and influence—she saw right through his aristocratic facade, down to the man beneath it.

Despite her initial reservations, Agatha had fallen for Lord Bart's softer side, the part of him he rarely showed to anyone. He was arrogant, but beneath the layers of arrogance was a man who wanted to be loved. And Agatha, in her infinite wisdom and compassion, had loved him. Truly. Deeply.

Lord Bart had never been so happy. Agatha transformed him, softening him in ways that unnerved his peers. For the first time, he questioned the rigid class boundaries he had always taken for granted. He no longer cared for his world's constant pretensions. All he wanted was Agatha.

After just a year of courtship, they were engaged, their wedding planned for a summer's day at Lord Bart's sprawling countryside estate. It was to be the event of the season—a grand affair filled with lords, ladies, and all the finery his wealth could afford. But Lord Bart hadn't cared about its grandeur at all. He only wanted to make Agatha his wife.

The night before the wedding, everything had been perfect. They had danced under the stars at an intimate dinner party, just the two laughing and talking about the future. Agatha had worn a pale blue dress that flowed around her like a dream, her dark hair cascading over her shoulders. She had never looked more beautiful to Lord Bart than she had that night.

But then, tragedy struck. On the way back to the manor, the car Lord Bart had purchased for her—a sleek, luxurious vehicle befitting his fiancée—skidded off the road during a sudden storm. The driver survived with only minor injuries, but Agatha was not so lucky. The crash had killed her instantly.

Lord Bart's world had crumbled in an instant. In a single moment, the future he had imagined with Agatha was gone, and he was left alone with nothing but memories and grief. He couldn't bear to face the pitying looks of his peers, the whispers that followed him wherever he went. He retreated from society, throwing himself into his collection of antiques, trying to fill the gaping void in his heart with relics from the past. But nothing—nothing—could bring her back.

Over the years, the sharp pain of Agatha's loss dulled into a constant ache. He had never loved again. How could he, when Agatha had been the only one who truly understood him? He carried her memory like a wound that never healed, buried beneath layers of wealth and arrogance.

And now, decades later, when Lord Bart had thought he had long since come to terms with her death, he found her again—in that dusty little shop, her face staring back at him from the picture frame.

The shopkeeper's voice slithered through the silence. "Ah, I see you've found something."

Lord Bart didn't respond. His eyes were fixed on the portrait, his mind spinning with long-forgotten memories. He had loved Agatha with a passion that had consumed him, and when she had been taken from him, something inside him had broken. He had never married after her death, never even courted another woman. She had been his everything.

"I'll take it," he said abruptly, his voice sharp with urgency. "Name your price."

"It's a rare piece, sir. Priceless, some might say," the shopkeeper smiled, her lips curling into something that resembled a sneer.

"Name your price!" Lord Bart barked, his voice rising.

The shopkeeper leaned forward, her dark eyes gleaming. "Oh, it's not about money, Lord Bart. But you've already paid in ways you cannot imagine."

Impatient and unnerved by her cryptic words, Lord Bart threw a wad of cash onto the counter. "Keep the change," he muttered before clutching the picture frame tightly and rushing out of the shop.

That night, Lord Bart lay in bed, the picture frame resting on the lampstand beside him. He stared at it for hours, his heart pounding as memories of Agatha flooded his mind. He remembered her laugh, the way she had looked at him with those soft, loving eyes. The way they had danced together under the stars, making plans for a future that had never come.

Eventually, exhaustion overtook him, and he fell into a restless sleep.

When he awoke the following day, something was different.

He sat up in bed, glancing around the room. Everything seemed... brighter. Sharper. He rubbed his eyes and swung his legs over the side of the bed. That's when he noticed it. His legs. They were strong and muscular—the legs of a young man. Lord Bart blinked in confusion. Once wrinkled and spotted with age, his hands were smooth and steady. He jumped to his feet, his heart racing as he stumbled to the bathroom mirror. The reflection staring back at him was not the old man he had become. It was him—but young, as he had been when Agatha was alive.

He turned and ran down the stairs, calling out in a voice that no longer trembled with age. "George? George!"

But when he reached the kitchen, it was not George who greeted him.

It was Agatha.

She stood at the stove, humming softly, her dark hair tied back in a loose bun, just as he remembered. She turned and smiled at him, the smile that had once lit up his world.

"Good morning, love," she said, her voice as soft and sweet as it had been all those years ago. "Breakfast will be ready soon."

Lord Bart's breath caught in his throat. "Agatha… is it really you?"

She laughed, a sound that sent shivers down his spine. "Of course it is, darling. Who else would it be?"

Tears filled his eyes as he crossed the room and embraced her. She was real. She was here. And for the first time in decades, Lord Bart felt alive again.

They spent the day reliving their happiest moments—walking through the manor's gardens, just as they had before. The sunlight filtered through the trees, casting golden light over them as they reminisced about their plans, dreams, and all the things they had never had a chance to do.

At dinner, they shared a bottle of wine, sitting across from each other at the grand table. The candles flickered between them, glowing warmly on Agatha's face. Lord Bart felt a peace he hadn't known in decades. It was as if everything had been set right again. Time had reversed, and they had been given a second chance.

They went to bed together that night, and for the first time in years, Lord Bart slept without the weight of grief pressing down on him. He dreamed of a future that had once been stolen from him—a future where they grew old together, side by side.

But when he awoke the following day, everything was back to normal.

He was old again. The manor was quiet. Agatha was gone. He was so distraught that he had an episode and had to be restrained by George.

The days that followed were a blur of confusion and despair. Each night, Lord Bart would fall asleep clutching the picture frame, and the following day, he would wake up young again, with Agatha by his side. But the next day, she would vanish, and reality would crash around him.

The pull of the dreams grew stronger each night. Agatha's presence became more intoxicating, more irresistible. It was everything Lord Bart had ever wanted—a world where Agatha was alive, they were happy, and time and death meant nothing.

But with each dream, something darker lurked at the edges. Agatha's once so pure smile began to flicker with something else—something unsettling. The perfect world they shared started to feel less like a reunion and more like a trap. Yet, Lord Bart couldn't stop himself. He needed her. He needed that world where his youth and love were restored.

One morning, however, it wasn't Agatha who greeted him. It was the shopkeeper. Her presence was suffocating, her eyes gleaming with a predatory hunger. She stood at the foot of his bed, her dark eyes glowing in the dim light.

"You want her, don't you?" she whispered, her voice a seductive hiss. "You want to be with Agatha forever."

Lord Bart nodded, his heart heavy with longing. "More than anything."

"You can be with her forever, you know," she said, her voice soft and menacing. "But there is a price."

Lord Bart stared at her, his heart pounding. "What do you mean?"

The shopkeeper smiled, her teeth sharp and white. "A life must be given, Lord Bart. A sacrifice. Only then will you be free to stay with her."

Lord Bart's blood ran cold. "A life? Whose life?"

The shopkeeper's smile widened. "Well, you're not exactly a social butterfly, so who else but your butler, George. He's served you faithfully, hasn't he? A life for a life, my lord. That is the cost."

Agatha's image flickered before his eyes, her soft smile, her gentle touch. How could he say no? How could he deny himself the only happiness he had ever known? But the thought of taking George's life gnawed at him, the guilt a festering wound in his mind.

Still, the dreams became too much. Each night with Agatha felt more real than the waking world, and Lord Bart's will crumbled. He was no longer a proud, arrogant man but a desperate one, clinging to the last threads of the life he had once dreamed of.

For days, Lord Bart wrestled with the decision. He couldn't bring himself to harm George, the one person who had stood by him through everything. But the temptation grew stronger with each passing night. The thought of being with Agatha again—forever—was more than he could bear.

In the end, the choice was inevitable. Lord Bart was willing to pay any price for the promise of love, youth, and happiness—even if it meant betraying the only person left in the real world who truly cared for him.

George noticed the change in his employer. Lord Bart became more agitated, erratic, and obsessed with the picture frame he had brought home from the strange thrift store. He began talking about Agatha again as if she were alive, as if he had seen her just the night before. At first, George thought it was just another symptom of Lord Bart's dementia, another heart-breaking delusion. But something about this time was different. There was a desperation in Lord Bart's eyes, a manic energy that George hadn't seen before.

As Lord Bart's mental state deteriorated, George became increasingly concerned. He stayed up at night, listening for any signs that Lord Bart might be wandering the house again. He tried to engage his employer in conversation, hoping to ground him in the present, but Lord Bart was distant, his mind elsewhere.

When Lord Bart began muttering about sacrifices and Agatha, George's concern deepened into fear. He could see that Lord Bart was being consumed by something darker than dementia—something far more insidious. George tried to stay close, to watch over Lord Bart as best he could, but there were moments when the old man's paranoia pushed him away.

One night, Lord Bart finally snapped. George had been preparing tea in the kitchen when Lord Bart appeared behind him, clutching a kitchen knife. At first, George didn't register the danger. He turned to speak to his employer, ready to calm him as he had done many times before. But the look in Lord Bart's eyes was different this time—wild, desperate, and terrifyingly focused. Before George could react, Lord Bart lunged, driven by the shopkeeper's promise that this act would reunite him with Agatha forever.

In his final moments, George's thoughts weren't of betrayal or anger. Instead, they were of pity. He had cared for

Lord Bart for so many years, had watched him fall apart piece by piece, and now, in this moment of horror, he saw only a man who had been broken by grief and madness. George had given his life to serving Lord Bart, and in the end, it had cost him everything.

Lord Bart returned to his room, clutching the picture frame to his chest, and lay down in bed with a smile on his face.

That night, he dreamed of Agatha. And he never woke up again.

REBIRTH

Marcel "M-Trel" Tyrell swayed slightly as he left the dimly lit club, the haze of cheap whiskey and marijuana clouding his mind. New Orleans, the pulsating city he grew up in, seemed to stand still. The night air was thick with the scent of distant rain, but Marcel didn't notice. His mind was elsewhere, back to the days when his name was everywhere—on the radio, on TV, in clubs, on the tongues of fans who worshipped him like a god. Now, no one even recognised him.

He stumbled past the flickering street lamps, hands shoved deep into his worn leather jacket pockets. His mind spun, not with inspiration but with bitterness. His first album had shot straight to the top of the charts, catapulting him into a life he wasn't prepared for. The mansion in Beverly Hills. The entourage. The endless stream of women and parties. But success came as quickly as it went, swallowed by two disastrous follow-up albums and a reckless lifestyle that led him to gun and drug charges. Two years in prison was the final nail in the coffin of his once-promising career.

He had been out of prison for six months, living in a run-down studio apartment in New Orleans, performing at dive bars and hole-in-the-wall clubs just to scrape by. And the $50,000 he thought would help him restart his career? That was gone too—stolen by his former promoter, who had him beaten and humiliated in the street, leaving him with nothing but a hundred-dollar bill and a shattered sense of self.

Now, all he had was his music—a fading dream—and the hope that he could prove to the world and himself that he wasn't washed up.

As Marcel stumbled through the empty streets, his attention was caught by something in the window of a small thrift store. A dusty and weathered old tuba gleamed faintly under the flickering streetlight. His steps faltered as he stared at it, a sudden wave of nostalgia washing over him. He remembered his father.

Marcel's father, Ernest Tyrell, was a legend in his own right, though he had never sought fame or fortune. A jazz musician born and raised in the heart of New Orleans, Ernest had lived his life by the rhythm of his convictions rather than the applause of an audience. His deep love for jazz wasn't just about the music but the story, heart, and soul that went into every note. In the smoky jazz clubs on Frenchmen Street, where the air was thick with the smell of bourbon and the hum of trumpets and saxophones, Ernest was a fixture. He never played to impress but always to express.

Ernest taught Marcel everything he knew about life, music, and the delicate balance between passion and pressure. He believed that music wasn't just a form of entertainment but a language—a way to communicate truths about the world and one's soul. For Ernest, being a musician wasn't about showing off skill or gaining fame. It was about speaking from the heart, even if nobody was listening.

"Son, music is like life," he used to say, his deep, raspy voice vibrating with the same richness as the low notes on his tuba. "It ain't about perfection. It's about finding the notes that resonate with who you are."

As a young boy, Marcel would sit cross-legged on the worn hardwood floor of their tiny living room, listening to his father play his tuba late into the night. Those sessions were a form of communion between father and son. Marcel would watch Ernest close his eyes as he played as if he were letting the music guide him rather than controlling it. It wasn't flashy but honest, raw, and powerful.

Ernest never made it big, though he easily could have. The jazz world had changed, and the opportunity to sell out and become a commercial success was always there. But Ernest was a man of principle. He turned down recording contracts, tours, and collaborations that didn't feel true to his art. That's what set him apart—not just his musical talent but his steadfast dedication to staying true to himself, even when it meant staying in the shadows of larger-than-life musicians.

As Marcel grew up, he rebelled against his father's way of thinking. The allure of fame and fortune, especially in the fast-paced world of hip-hop, was hard to resist. Marcel didn't want to live in a cramped apartment in the Ninth Ward forever, scraping by on passion alone. He wanted more—the glitz, the glamour, the money. He wanted to be seen. He wanted to be known. And when his first album exploded onto the scene, it felt like everything was falling into place. The fame, the parties, the attention—it was intoxicating.

But Ernest's words had always lingered in the back of his mind, even as Marcel spiralled into the excesses of celebrity life.

"You can't fake the funk forever, son," Ernest had warned him once after watching Marcel perform a show that was more about pyrotechnics than poetry. "You might fool the crowd, but you can't fool yourself."

At the time, Marcel had brushed it off, too caught up in the high of his newfound fame. But now, as he stood at the crossroads of his career, his father's words echoed louder than ever. Marcel had strayed far from the lessons Ernest had tried to instil in him. The fame he had chased had only led him down a dark path.

Ernest had passed away a few years before Marcel hit rock bottom. The heart attack had come suddenly, taking the old man from a world he had always observed with a wry, knowing smile. Marcel hadn't been there when it happened. He had been on tour thousands of miles away, performing for a sold-out stadium. By the time he got the news, his father was already gone. The guilt of not being there, of not heeding his father's wisdom when he was alive—haunted Marcel like a ghost.

Seeing that tuba felt like seeing his father again, a ghost from his past calling out to him. Without thinking, Marcel turned and walked into the store.

The door creaked open, and as he entered, he nearly collided with an elderly gentleman who was rushing out. The man clutched a picture frame to his chest, his eyes wild, and he didn't even acknowledge Marcel as he shoved past him. Marcel muttered under his breath, irritated, but the strange encounter faded from his mind as he stepped further into the dimly lit store.

The place was cluttered with antiques and oddities belonging to a different time. Behind the counter stood a mysterious storekeeper, her dark eyes gleaming in the shadows. She greeted him with a slow, knowing smile, which welcomed Marcel. He walked up to her and engaged in small talk.

"What is it you do?" she asked with piercing eyes.

"I spit rhymes, at least I used to," he responded cynically.

"A poet?" she asked.

"A rapper, M-Trel," he said, hoping she would recognise the name. He was disappointed when she didn't.

"I have something that should spark your interest." She goes to the back of the store and returns with a beatmaker.

It was old, the kind of beatmaker he hadn't seen in years, but something about it intrigued him—something... familiar.

"You like that, don't you?" the woman said, her voice soft but sharp, cutting through the fog in his mind. Marcel blinked, looking up at her.

"Yeah... What is that?" he asked, his voice hoarse from the night's performance.

"That," she said, "once belonged to the greatest musician since the dawn of time. Who, like you, fell from glory. But this beatmaker... it can give you your power back."

Marcel laughed bitterly. "Lady, I ain't got the money for that."

The woman's smile widened. "You don't need money. Just give me a performance. Recite a poem for me, and the beatmaker is yours.

Marcel hesitated, looking at the beatmaker. His heart raced, the alcohol and weed amplifying his curiosity and desperation. "A poem, huh? What's the catch?"

"No catch," the woman said. "But you'll need two words to guide your poem: dream and eternity."

Marcel stood there for a moment, the words swirling in his mind. Then, almost instinctively, he began to speak.

"Dreams, they come, and they fade,

Like echoes in the midnight shade.

But eternity, it never bends,

It's where the dream begins and ends.

Lost in the haze of life's long scheme,

Chasing the truth of an endless dream."

The room seemed to hum with energy as he spoke, and when he finished, the woman clapped softly, her eyes gleaming with something he couldn't quite place.

"Very good," she said. "The beatmaker is yours."

Marcel hesitated for a moment but then took the beatmaker from her hands. As he turned to leave, the door opened, and he held it for a teenage girl who was just entering. She was soaking wet even though it wasn't raining outside, but Marcel barely noticed. He was already thinking about the beatmaker in his hands.

When he returned to his apartment, Marcel set the beatmaker up on his cluttered desk. It looked ancient, but as he plugged it in and powered it up, it whirred to life with a strange hum. He sat down, staring at the device, unsure what to expect. The clock ticked toward midnight, and the rest of the world outside his window fell silent. Something about the beatmaker felt different in that hour—a strange hum, almost alive, pulsed through it.

He shrugged off the unease, thinking it was just his mind playing tricks on him. He lit a joint to calm his nerves and started tapping keys, playing around with the machine. But as soon as his fingers hit the pads, something shifted. His thoughts, which had been cluttered with doubts, frustrations, and a crushing sense of failure, melted away. He felt a strange calmness wash over him like the air in the room thickened and slowed down. Then, a sudden surge of energy. Something took over his body. His mind went blank, and everything around him faded. At first, he wasn't aware of it. His fingers moved independently, a rhythm emerging from the beatmaker that he couldn't remember programming. His surroundings blurred—the small, dingy apartment seemed to dissolve, and suddenly, he was standing in the middle of a recording studio much larger than the ones he'd ever worked in. The walls were panelled with sleek, dark wood, and golden lights bathed the space in an otherworldly glow. The air was charged with the energy of creation.

In front of him, faceless musicians sat with instruments—keyboards, drums, guitars—but their hands never moved. The music, a haunting beat with layers of melody and bass, pulsed through the room as if it had always been there, and Marcel was merely tuning into it. Sound engineers stood behind a massive glass panel, tweaking knobs and pushing buttons, though their faces were obscured, blurred as if they were from a memory he couldn't fully recall. It was like the outlines of reality had softened, and this dreamlike place was waiting for him to create.

A microphone stood tall in the centre of the room, waiting for him. Marcel stepped up to it without thinking, words flowing through his mind before he even opened his mouth. The beat pounded in his chest, pulling something deep from within him, but the lyrics were strange, almost foreign. He rapped, but the words weren't his own—they came from a place he didn't recognise. It was darker, sharper, and commercial in a way that he'd always despised but couldn't resist. The verses were flawless, the cadence perfect, but they didn't reflect the struggle, pain, or truth he usually put into his music.

It was a version of himself, but not him. It was something manufactured, polished, almost too perfect.

When the trance finally broke, Marcel found himself slumped over his desk, his hands still resting on the beatmaker. His heart was racing, and sweat dripped from his forehead. For a moment, he didn't remember what had just happened. The room was quiet again, save for the hum of his computer.

He sat up and blinked, looking at the screen. There it was—an entire track recorded, a song that hadn't existed an hour ago but now played back in crisp detail. He hit play, listening to the product of the trance. The song was good. In fact, it was incredible. His flow was immaculate, the lyrics sharp and deep, the hook was catchy, the beat was perfect, and the production was slick. It sounded like something that would dominate the airwaves, a track that would shoot straight to the top of the charts.

But it didn't sound like him. It was polished in a way that made him uneasy. The lyrics, though captivating, were darker than anything he'd ever written. They dripped with aggression, manipulation, and materialism, themes he had always pushed back against. Where was the heart? Where was the soul? And yet... it was so good.

He listened to the song again. Then again. And by the third time, he wasn't questioning it anymore. He was hooked.

The following night, just before midnight, he sat back at the beatmaker. A part of him was hesitant, remembering how disconnected he'd felt from the music afterwards. He remembered his father's words, which had guided him through the early days of his career: "Stay true to yourself, son. The moment you lose yourself in this game, it's over."

But another part of him, the part that longed for success and recognition, itched to do it again. He wanted to chase that perfection. He wanted to feel that rush, that power, that flawless creativity.

And so, as the clock struck midnight, he began. Again, the room shifted. He was transported back into the dream studio, surrounded by faceless musicians and sound engineers who worked with precision, though their forms remained blurred. This time, there was no hesitation. He stepped up to the microphone, letting the music take over him. He rapped, but the words felt distant, almost like someone else was speaking through him. But it was perfect—every rhyme, every beat hit precisely where it should. The lyrics poured out, one verse after another, telling a story that wasn't his, but still... it was brilliant.

When he woke from the trance, another song sat waiting on his screen. This one was even better than the last—tighter, more complex, with a darker edge that made it both commercial and provocative. He listened to it on repeat, loving it and hating it all at once. The music was fire, but its soul was cold.

As the nights went on, the trances grew more intense. The studio setting became more surreal, more dreamlike. The blurred faces of the musicians and engineers began to take on a ghostly quality, like shadows that moved in rhythm with the music but lacked any real substance. Marcel felt disconnected from the process, as though he were watching someone else perform in his place, someone who looked like him but wasn't truly him.

With each new track, the music became darker, more twisted, as if the beatmaker was pulling him deeper into an abyss. The lyrics spoke of pain, betrayal, and emptiness, themes Marcel had touched on before but had never fully embraced. Now, they consumed him. The words he spits into the microphone feel foreign as if they were coming from some other part of his mind, a part he barely recognises. He would finish a track and listen to it back, marvelling at how polished and perfect it was, yet feeling a hollow pit grow in his stomach.

There was a sinister undercurrent to the music. The rhythms were hypnotic, pulling him in, but the message was cold, detached, like the person who had written the lyrics wasn't concerned with life or love but with something darker—something more dangerous. Marcel didn't know who he was becoming but couldn't stop. The beatmaker had him in its grip. He was addicted to the high of creating, even if what he created terrified him.

Yet the allure of the success these songs could bring was too powerful to ignore. He began sending the tracks to his old industry contacts, and the responses were immediate. Labels were interested. Promoters were calling. The songs were undeniably good, and it looked like Marcel was about to make his comeback. The buzz around his name grew with each passing day.

But with every new track he recorded in a trance, he felt more empty, more disconnected from the person he once was. The songs had become his ticket back to fame and fortune but at the cost of his soul. He couldn't shake the feeling that something dark was creeping into his life, something born from that beatmaker and the trance it brought on. And yet, he kept going, driven by the desperate need to prove he wasn't washed up.

The trance, though seductive, was draining him, turning him into something unrecognisable, both in his music and his life. His soul was slipping away with every note, every lyric, and every night spent in that dream world.

Within months, Marcel had signed a new contract, and his comeback album,

Rebirth, was topping the charts globally. His name was on everyone's lips again. He was hounded for endorsements and collaborations. He moved into a new mansion in Beverly Hills and reclaimed the fame and fortune he had lost.

The more success he gained, the more he felt like a stranger in his own skin. He couldn't recognise himself anymore—the person staring back at him in the mirror was someone else, someone hollow and lost. His once hardcore persona was now watered down with brightly-coloured clothes and nail polish. The music was good, but it wasn't 'his' music. And with every passing day, he felt more disconnected from the world around him, as if the very essence of who he was had been drained away.

Marcel sat in his studio with the lights dimmed low, the beatmaker's glow casting long shadows across the room. It had been over a year since the album dropped, and the world had again crowned him king. But inside, something was broken. The fame, the applause, the money—it all felt hollow. He placed his hands on the beatmaker, the machine humming beneath his fingers as if it had a life of its own. A deep sense of unease gnawed at him, and his chest tightened with the weight of his decisions. Still, he needed to start working on his next album.

As the clock struck midnight, he closed his eyes. He felt his surroundings shift again. This time, it wasn't the blurred musicians or faceless engineers that surrounded him. Instead, he found himself back in the cramped, smoke-filled clubs of his early days, the ones where he had honed his craft. The air was thick with the smell of sweat, smoke, and alcohol. People filled the small space, but like the musicians, their faces were obscured. They were watching him, waiting for him to perform, to deliver something raw, something real.

But Marcel couldn't find the words. His mouth opened, but nothing came out. The crowd grew restless, their murmurs rising into a cacophony of impatience. Marcel's heart pounded in his chest. He had always prided himself on being able to spit bars on command, but now, in this strange, dreamlike setting, he was paralysed. The beatmaker was in front of him, glowing faintly as if urging him to tap into its power once again.

In the distance, a single spotlight flickered, illuminating two figures. One was his father. Tall, steady, with the wise and weathered look of a man who had seen the world for what it was. His tuba rested at his side, a testament to his years of dedication to jazz and the craft he had lived and died for. The other figure was him—his alter ego, the version of himself that had climbed back to the top of the charts, eyes glinting with confidence, dressed in designer clothes, dripping in gold and diamonds.

It was a trialogue, a battle for Marcel's soul, between his father's wisdom and the seductive promises of his alter ego.

"You're torn, Marcel," his alter ego began, a grin playing on his lips. "But you shouldn't be. Look around you, man. You've made it. You were born to entertain, to be idolised and praised. You deserve the fame and fortune. You've earned it!"

Marcel looked at him, his alter ego radiating success, confidence, and power. His words echoed the thoughts Marcel had tried to suppress. Maybe he was right. Perhaps he was born for this life—the life of applause, fans screaming his name, private jets, and flashing lights. It had been a struggle to get back to the top, but why would he give it all up now that he was there?

But then, his father's voice cut through the haze like a clarinet in a smoky jazz club.

"An entertainer is driven by compulsion, Marcel, but an artist... an artist is driven by conviction." His father's eyes were steady, filled with a kind of truth that pierced through Marcel's uncertainty. "An entertainer's primary audience is the crowd, but an artist's primary audience is himself."

Marcel's heart tightened. He had heard these words from his father before when he was just a kid learning to rhyme. He had taught Marcel the difference between chasing the spotlight and sharing something real. Back then, it had made sense. Now, after all the fame, years lost to reckless living, and the need to survive, those words seemed almost naive.

"You're not an entertainer," his father continued, his voice unwavering. "You're an artist. And that's who you were always meant to be. Don't lose yourself in the noise."

Marcel's gaze shifted between his father and his alter ego, caught between two worlds. The alter ego stepped forward, his gold chain clinking with every movement. He epitomised what Marcel thought he wanted to be—untouchable, adored, powerful.

"You hear that old man?" his alter ego sneered. "That's the voice of someone who never made it to the top. Someone who never tasted what real success feels like. Look at yourself, Marcel! You've got everything now! The world knows your name again. You're living the life others would kill for. Do you think being an artist matters when you've got bills to pay? When you've got people begging for more of you?"

"Calmly yet firmly, his father continued, "Like a shooting star, an entertainer fades away quickly, but an artist's legacy lives for generations after he's gone."

His alter ego leaned closer, his voice soft but dangerous, like a snake hissing in the grass. "Forget about 'staying true to yourself.' That's just some idealistic nonsense. You were born for this, to have everything—fame, fortune, power. Don't throw it all away over some romantic notion of 'authenticity.' You know what you really are? You're an entertainer. You give the people what they want, and they'll keep you on top. Isn't that what you've always dreamed of?"

Marcel's mind raced. He had been fighting this inner battle for a long time, torn between the fame he craved and his lost sense of self. His father had always warned him about this, about the seductive nature of success. And yet, the temptation to stay in the limelight was overwhelming. He felt its pull like a gravitational force.

But his father's voice cut through again, gentle but firm. "Being true to yourself isn't a 'romantic notion,' son. It's your anchor. It's what keeps you grounded in a world that'll chew you up and spit you out the moment you give in. Don't mistake applause for validation. The crowd? They'll move on to the next big thing when you stop giving them what they want. But if you stay true to who you are, your art will last. It will mean something. Even if it's just to you."

Marcel closed his eyes, the weight of the decision crushing down on him. His alter ego's words rang true—he had made it again. His name was back in lights, and the world had embraced him like he had never left. But deep down, something about it felt... wrong. Every time he listened to his new tracks, something felt hollow, like he wasn't even the one making the music. He was just a puppet, moving to the beat of someone else's drum.

"I've been where you are," his father continued, his voice softening. "I've seen what happens when you lose sight of what's important. Success fades, but who you are—that's forever. Don't let them take that away from you."

The stage grew darker as his alter ego laughed, his voice bouncing off the walls. "You're stuck in the past, old man! Marcel's a legend now. He's on top of the world. And you want him to walk away from all that? From everything he's worked for? Don't listen to him, Marcel. You don't need to be a tortured artist to make great music. You've earned this. You deserve every bit of it. You've fought for it. Take what's yours and ride it until the wheels fall off."

The words stung Marcel like a slap in the face. He was torn in two, standing at the crossroads of his soul. His father's wisdom felt like a guiding light, reminding him of the boy who started rhyming in the streets of New Orleans, driven by something pure. But his alter ego? He was everything Marcel had wanted to be—rich, famous, adored. The world had told him he wasn't washed up and could still be a king. But at what cost?

Marcel felt the weight of the beatmaker in his hand, its hum pulsating through him. It had given him everything back, but at the same time, it had stolen something essential: his identity, his truth.

"Son," his father's voice echoed softly, "an entertainer gives the people what they want, but an artist gives them what he has. And you, Marcel, you have something real to give. Don't lose that."

With that, his father and alter ego said in unison, "The choice is yours." The stage began to fade, and the lights dimmed until everything went black.

When Marcel opened his eyes, he was back in his studio, the beatmaker still humming softly in his hands. He leaned back in his chair, tears streaming down his face. He screamed and cried until his throat hurt.

After crying, he poured himself a drink from the $45,000 bottle of cognac on the table, rolled a blunt, lit it, and reclined his chair. He spent the night in the studio drinking and smoking, trying to drown and choke out his pain.

The bottle was empty by morning, and ash littered the studio floor. The choice was clear now—painful but clear.

Without another word, Marcel stood, grabbed the beatmaker, and smashed it against the wall. The device shattered, pieces scattering across the room. The finality of the act hit him like a tidal wave. The shards of plastic and metal lay scattered across the floor of his studio, a visual representation of his broken career, his shattered dreams, and the ghosts he had been chasing for far too long.

For a moment, he stood there in the silence that followed, his hands trembling from the force of his decision. His heart pounded, but it wasn't the erratic rhythm of panic or regret—it was something more profound, more peaceful. It was relief.

He took a deep breath, inhaling the room's stale air, which now felt like a prison he had finally escaped. His fingers loosened their grip, and he let the last fragment of the beatmaker slip through his hands and clatter to the floor. This machine—this cursed device—had consumed him, dictated his life, and turned his art into a soulless pursuit of fame and fortune. But now, it was gone. He was done with it all.

Through the night, the trialogue unfolded in Marcel's mind. His father stood as the voice of reason, the conscience Marcel had lost touch with in his pursuit of fame. With its seductive power, the beatmaker represented everything Ernest had warned him about—the danger of losing oneself in the crowd's noise. Marcel's alter ego, dripping in wealth and success, was the manifestation of the fame Marcel had chased, but it was hollow, empty, and without substance.

Ultimately, Ernest's words cut through the confusion. Marcel knew his father was right. Fame and fortune had brought him nothing but emptiness, and now he could reclaim what mattered—his truth, voice, and art. It was time to walk away from the crowd and rediscover the artist within.

He walked away from the studio, leaving the wreckage behind. Not once, looking back.

That morning, Marcel packed a single duffel bag. He didn't need much—just the essentials: some clothes, his wallet, a notebook, and an old photograph of his father, Ernest, standing in front of Preservation Hall with his tuba slung over his shoulder. It was the only thing that mattered now. Music wasn't something to be exploited or sold to the highest bidder. It was supposed to be an expression of who he was, and he had lost sight of that. His father had known it all along.

With no fanfare and no goodbye, Marcel left Los Angeles. He walked away from the industry, the nightclubs, and the man he had become. The city that had embraced him, that had once been the source of his inspiration, now felt foreign. It was time to find something new, to go somewhere quiet, where the world's noise wouldn't drown out the voice in his heart.

He went home to Louisiana, to a small, peaceful town where the only music he heard was the sound of the wind through the trees and the distant hum of the bayou.

Marcel settled into a simple life. He worked odd jobs as a handyman, helping at local farms and spending evenings on the porch, strumming a beat-up old guitar he had found in a pawn shop. He hadn't played guitar in years—his focus had always been on rapping, creating beats and lyrics that resonated with the streets. But now, with nothing to prove, he rediscovered the joy of playing music for himself. There was no audience, no critics, just him and the music.

The locals didn't recognise him, and he didn't bother to tell them who he was. To them, he was just Marcel, the quiet man who fixed fences and helped repair roofs. Occasionally, people would invite him over for a beer or a barbeque, and slowly, he became a part of the community. It wasn't the life he had imagined, but it was real. And for the first time in years, he was happy.

Music was still a part of his life, but it was no longer an obsession. Marcel played because he loved it, because it connected him to something deeper. He wrote songs not for the charts but for himself. Simple songs, songs about life, loss, love, and redemption. He didn't need anyone else to hear them. He wasn't looking for approval or validation. The music was for him, and that was enough.

Months passed, and Marcel began to feel whole again. The dark clouds that had hung over him for so long started to lift. The demons of fame and fortune no longer haunted him. The pressure to succeed, to be something he wasn't, had dissipated. He wasn't the washed-up rapper clinging to a fading dream anymore. He was just a man, living on his own terms, at peace with himself.

Sometimes, he would look up at the stars late at night and think about the life he had left behind. The lights, money, and adoring fans seemed like a distant memory, a dream belonging to someone else. He had tasted the highs of success and endured the crushing lows of failure, but now, standing under the vast Louisiana sky, he realised that none of it had ever mattered.

What mattered was here, in this quiet place, with the simple life he had chosen for himself. What mattered was staying true to himself as an artist, not an entertainer. His father had been right all along. An artist's primary audience was himself. And now, Marcel had finally learned to listen.

One evening, as the sun set over the horizon, Marcel sat on his porch with his guitar. He began to play, his fingers moving effortlessly over the strings. The music flowed out of him, soft and sweet, like a gentle breeze. He wasn't thinking about it, wasn't trying to force it. It was just there, inside him, waiting to be released.

For the first time in a long time, Marcel smiled. He had found his peace, his purpose. He didn't need fame or fortune to validate who he was. He was an artist. And that was enough.

THE GIRL BEHIND THE VEIL

Binta was born in a small village in the Mambilla Plateau in northeastern Nigeria. The plateau was a paradise with its rolling hills, lush greenery, and cool breezes. Her childhood days were filled with adventure, climbing trees with her friends, racing barefoot through the grass, and listening to the birds' melodic songs. The nights, however, were her favourite. Gathered around a crackling fire under a tapestry of stars, her mother told stories—ancient folklore passed down from generation to generation. Her mother's voice was smooth and lyrical, weaving tales of talking animals, tricksters, and spirits.

But of all the stories, Binta most cherished the ones about the Marsh Harrier. Her mother described the bird in vivid detail: its wingspan broad and strong, gliding high above the plateau, watching over the land with a protective gaze. The bird would fly to distant lands but always returned home, as if the plateau itself called it back. Binta would close her eyes, imagining herself soaring through the skies like the majestic Harrier, free and unburdened, looking down on the beauty of her homeland.

Her father, a farmer, worked their ancestral land with the kind of pride that came from generations of ownership. He taught her the importance of the earth and of tending to the crops that sustained them. Life in the village was simple but fulfilling, and Binta never imagined it could change.

But everything did change when she was ten. The growing tensions between local farmers and nomadic herders exploded into violence one fateful night. Her village was attacked, and the serene world she knew crumbled into chaos. Screams filled the air, smoke rose in the distance, and Binta's family was dragged from their home. Her father fought back, trying to protect them, but he was struck down in front of her eyes. Her mother was next, her beautiful voice silenced forever. Then, her siblings, all five of them. Binta, too young and too small to defend herself, was left scarred both inside and out, her innocence brutally stolen by the men who left her for dead.

She awoke hours later, alone, the village in ruins. Her face bore a deep, jagged scar, a permanent reminder of the night that shattered her world. With no family left, nowhere to turn, and nothing but horror in her heart, she made her way to an Internally Displaced Persons (IDP) camp, where survival was just as brutal as the attack.

For two years, Binta endured the bleak reality of life in the camp. Food and water were scarce, sanitation was non-existent, and the stench of death and misery hung in the air. The men in the camp, including the officials who were supposed to help, preyed on the weak, and Binta was not spared. The constant threat of violence followed her even in the supposed safety of the camp, where her scarred face made her a target for cruelty. Every night, she relived the horrors of her village, the faces of her murdered family haunting her dreams.

During one of these dark days, she met Louise Beauvais, a French aid worker with a soft voice and kind eyes. Louise saw something in Binta that no one else did: a spark of life that had not yet been extinguished. Louise took Binta in as her own daughter, adopting her and bringing her to Paris, far from the terrors of northern Nigeria. But with its bustling streets and foreign language, Paris was a world so vastly different from the Mambilla Plateau. Binta felt lost.

Paris was cold, both literally and metaphorically. Her scar made her a subject of whispers and mockery, especially among the children at school. They taunted her, calling her names and pointing at her face. Even as she grew older, the bullying never truly stopped. Binta always wore a scarf, using it as a shield, an armour against the stares. Only in the privacy of her bedroom did she take it off, staring into the mirror at the stranger reflected back at her.

The scarf gave her the ability to hide from the world's scrutiny. Her scar was a constant reminder of her trauma, inviting cruel stares and judgment. With the scarf, she could cover her scar and retreat into anonymity, finding solace in the idea that people would no longer see her as 'damaged'. It offered her a sense of safety, a barrier between her and a world that had been nothing but hostile.

Louise was always supportive, taking Binta to counselling and doing everything to help her heal. But no amount of treatment could erase the pain, the anger, and the deep sense of injustice that had taken root inside Binta. Despite Louise's love, Binta felt alone, her self-worth buried beneath the weight of her trauma.

By the time she turned eighteen, Binta had lost Louise as well. Louise was killed while on a humanitarian mission in northeastern

Nigeria—tragically, the very place where she had rescued Binta from. The loss was a cruel reminder of the world Binta had tried to leave behind, and now, once again, she found herself alone. Louise's death left her with the small two-bedroom apartment above a pastry shop and the shop itself, a modest inheritance that felt like a lifeline but also a burden.

One cold, rainy evening, as she returned from a counselling session, a gust blew Binta's scarf away. The rain started to pour as she chased the scarf down the street, watching helplessly as it landed on the roof of a small store. Soaked and desperate, she stepped into the store, seeking shelter and something to cover her face.

Inside, the storekeeper who ran the shop approached her. Binta tried to hide her scar, but the woman gently took her hands and lowered them. Something was unsettling yet comforting in the woman's touch. As they talked, Binta found herself opening up about her past—the attack, the camp, the scar that made her feel like less than a person.

The storekeeper listened in silence and then offered her a beautiful black embroidered face veil, telling Binta that it would protect her from harm but that she must wear it every day and take it off each night.

The storekeeper's words—"No one will ever hurt you again"—resonated deeply with her, as Binta had been hurt repeatedly, both physically and emotionally. Even if it came at a strange cost, the idea of being shielded from further pain was too enticing to resist.

The face veil had intricate black embroidery and a delicate design. Unlike other face coverings she had worn in the past to hide her scar, this veil felt different—like it was made for her. Its allure was not simply in its ability to conceal her face, but in the strange promise of protection the storekeeper offered.

The veil seemed like a lifeline. It promised her something she had craved for years: safety from the stares, the judgment, and the constant feeling of being an outsider. More than that, it symbolised a way to hide from the world, to escape the endless vulnerability she felt every day. It wasn't just about covering her physical scar; it was also a response to her emotional wounds. She had felt powerless for so long—unable to control what had happened to her, unable to change how the world saw her. The veil seemed like a magical solution, a way to regain a sense of control over her life, and it played into her desire to feel invisible yet powerful, to protect herself without confronting her inner demons.

Desperate for peace, Binta accepted the veil. The rain had become a drizzle, so she wore the veil and went home.

For the first time in years, she slept without nightmares and sleep paralysis. But when she awoke, something strange had happened: a man's wedding band sat on her nightstand. A deep sense of unease washed over her. At first, she blinked, staring at the shiny, small ring with confusion, wondering if her tired mind was playing tricks on her. The wedding band sat there, out of place yet undeniable in its presence, glinting under the soft morning light. She felt a chill run down her spine, her body tensing as though something was terribly wrong, even though the room around her was quiet and still.

Her first instinct was disbelief. She didn't remember having the band or knowing anyone who would have left such a personal item. Her hands trembled as she reached out and touched it, the cold metal sending a shock through her fingertips. Binta felt the weight of something sinister she couldn't yet comprehend. She looked around the room, trying to understand how it had appeared next to her bed. Her mind raced back to the moment she accepted the veil, to the old storekeeper's cryptic words. There had been a sense of relief in finally feeling protected, but now, staring at the wedding band, she felt a different kind of fear creeping in.

Her breath quickened. Questions filled her mind: Whose was this? Why was it here? What had happened while she slept? The once comforting sense of safety the veil had given her began to crumble as the band's mystery gnawed at her. There was something deeply unsettling about waking up to this intimate, unexplainable object. It was as if a stranger had been in her space, her dreams, without her knowledge.

A cold sweat broke out across her skin, and Binta instinctively reached for the veil hanging nearby. For the first time, instead of comfort, she felt a creeping dread about what wearing it might mean. The band in her hand was more than just a piece of metal—it was a warning, a symbol of something dark unfolding, something she had yet to understand fully.

Binta woke each morning to find a new item on her nightstand, and her feelings of unease deepened. After the wedding band, she was desperate to believe it had been a one-time anomaly, a strange coincidence she could brush aside. But her unease morphed into outright fear when she woke up to find a wristwatch the next day, followed by a bracelet, a keychain, and a lighter on subsequent mornings.

With each new item, the questions became louder in her mind, and the pit in her stomach grew heavier. Where were these things coming from? How were they getting here? She hadn't brought them into her apartment, hadn't seen them before, and certainly hadn't been expecting to find them next to her bed.

The wristwatch had felt strange but not yet terrifying—just a small, ordinary thing she could have picked up somewhere. But she felt a deep shiver when she found the bracelet, a delicate piece with initials engraved on the clasp. It was personal and intimate, like the wedding band. And when she saw the keychain and lighter, both with worn details and signs of extended use, the horror inside her swelled. These weren't random objects; they belonged to someone.

Each item felt heavier than the last, as though the weight of their origin was slowly suffocating her. Binta would lie awake at night, afraid to fall asleep, dreading what she might find next. She began to fear her dreams and what was happening while sleeping. The veil, once a source of protection, had become a prison. She felt trapped in a waking nightmare, unsure of what was real, uncertain if she was somehow responsible for these items appearing.

With every object, the veil felt more sinister, more cursed. Her sense of reality blurred—was she the one bringing these items into her home? Did she know these people? The items became symbols of a dark secret she couldn't access, a part of herself that was acting without her knowledge. And worst of all, they felt like silent accusations, as though each item whispered that something terrible was happening—and she was at the centre.

Then, one morning, she woke up and saw a wallet. This was the breaking point. It was no longer something she could ignore or dismiss. She sat up in bed, her hands shaking as she opened it, her heart pounding in her chest. It wasn't just a wallet filled with cash—business cards, a driver's license, and personal photos were tucked inside. It was an identity. A man's life reduced to the contents of this wallet and now inexplicably on her nightstand.

Binta decided to track down the owner of the wallet. She was both terrified and determined. She couldn't ignore the gnawing feeling that something sinister was happening far beyond her comprehension. The items piling up in her small apartment had weighed too heavily on her mind. With its clear-cut evidence of a person's identity, the wallet felt like her only chance to get to the bottom of it.

After sitting on the floor of her bedroom for what felt like hours, staring at the driver's license and the business cards, she finally took a deep breath and resolved to find the man. The name on the cards was a clear lead: **Armand Laurent**, printed in sharp letters, along with an office address. She clutched the wallet tightly, knowing she needed to follow through with this despite her pounding heart.

It was raining that day as she ventured out of her apartment, the grey sky mirroring the dread she carried inside. Binta barely noticed the cold wind biting at her skin. She boarded the metro and rode silently, staring at the wallet, replaying the moments when these bizarre items had appeared. She kept thinking about the veil and the strange, peaceful sleep it brought her. Now, she began to wonder if her restful nights were a sign of something more terrifying—like she was completely losing control of herself.

She hesitated at the entrance when she reached the office building, an upscale glass-fronted structure. What if the man recognised the wallet? What if he had been missing it and could explain everything? Or worse—What if something terrible had already happened to him?

She entered the lobby with shaky steps, clutching the business card in one hand. The receptionist behind the front desk glanced up from her computer and smiled politely, though her eyes quickly darted to the veil covering Binta's face. Binta nervously adjusted it, her fingers trembling.

"Good afternoon," Binta said, her voice barely above a whisper as she handed over the business card. "I'm here to see Mr. Armand Laurent. Is he in today?"

The receptionist's expression shifted from polite indifference to something more cautious. "I'm sorry," she said slowly. "Mr. Laurent... he passed away last night."

The words hit Binta like a sucker punch. Her mind reeled. "Passed away?" Her mouth went dry, and she struggled to keep her breathing steady.

"Passed away?" she stammered. "How? What happened?"

Before the receptionist could respond, two detectives stepped out of a nearby office. With sharp eyes and a calm demeanour, the female detective saw Binta holding the business card.

"Excuse me," the detective said, approaching. "Can we help you? How do you know Mr. Laurent?"

Binta's heart pounded in her chest, her thoughts racing. She had no idea what to say. Already rattled, her fear only deepened when these officers confronted her.

"He... came into my shop yesterday," Binta lied quickly. "He... forgot his wallet, and I just thought to return it."

The male detective raised an eyebrow, clearly unconvinced. "What's the name of your shop?" he asked, suspicion dripping from his tone.

"It's a pastry shop," she stammered. "On Rue de la Victoire."

The female detective exchanged a glance with her partner. "Mr. Laurent was murdered last night," she said quietly, studying Binta's reaction. "We're trying to piece together what happened."

Binta felt like the floor was giving way beneath her. "Murdered?" Her fingers tightened around the wallet, her pulse roaring in her ears.

"I don't know anything about that," she managed to say. "I'm just here to return his wallet. He must have... dropped it."

The detectives were silent for a long moment, the weight of their suspicion heavy in the air.

"Can you come down to the station with us?" the female detective asked. "Just for some questions. We need to make sure we have everything clear."

Binta nodded numbly, feeling trapped. She didn't know how to explain her connection to the wallet or the other items without sounding completely insane. The realisation that she was now entangled in something far darker than she had anticipated settled like a stone in her chest.

As she followed the detectives out of the office building and into the rain-soaked streets, Binta felt the veil on her face clinging to her skin, an oppressive weight she couldn't shake. Something was very wrong, but she had no idea how to unravel the mystery of what was happening to her—or how deep it went.

Binta sat in the cold, sterile interrogation room at the police station, the sound of the rain still echoing faintly in her ears. The fluorescent light buzzed overhead, casting a harsh glow on the metal table in front of her. Her fingers fidgeted nervously, and she tugged at the edges of her veil, which was slightly damp from the rain. The veil had been her shield for years, and now, sitting in this room, she felt more exposed than ever.

The two detectives who had escorted her to the station entered the room quietly, their eyes fixed on her. The female detective,

Detective Moreau, carried a folder under her arm, while the male detective, Detective Caron, leaned against the wall, arms crossed, his eyes sharp and watchful. Their demeanour wasn't aggressive, but the air was thick with suspicion.

"Miss Binta, thank you for coming with us," Detective Moreau began as she sat across from her, opening the folder. Her voice was calm but probing. We just have a few questions about your connection to Armand Laurent. You said you last saw him in your pastry shop. Is that correct?"

"Yes," Binta replied quietly, her voice tight. "He… came in briefly. He left his wallet by accident. That's why I was trying to return it."

Moreau nodded slowly, flipping through her notes. "But you didn't try to call him?"

"I—" Binta faltered, feeling the weight of their suspicion pressing down on her. She hadn't called. She didn't even know what she had intended to do until she ended up at his office.

"It's strange, though," Detective Caron cut in, his voice slightly more direct. "Mr Laurent was found dead last night. And you happen to show up today with his wallet. Why didn't you report it sooner?"

Binta felt a tightening in her chest. She tried to explain but felt the words stick in her throat. How could she tell them about the strange way the wallet had appeared? That every night she woke up with more mysterious items left behind by murdered men?

"I—I didn't know," she whispered, keeping her eyes down. "I just wanted to return it. I didn't know he was…"

Moreau leaned forward, her gaze softening slightly. "Miss Binta, we understand this is a lot to take in, but you must help us understand what's happening. Why would Mr. Laurent have left his wallet with you if he didn't intend to return?"

Binta opened her mouth to speak but couldn't find an answer. The truth was impossible to explain.

Caron's gaze flickered toward her veil, a look of curiosity crossing his face. "You're hiding something," he said suddenly, his voice low but piercing. "What's with the veil?"

Binta stiffened, her hands instinctively flying to the edges of the fabric, clutching it tightly. "It's nothing," she said quickly, her voice shaky. "Just a veil."

Caron stepped forward, his expression growing more intense. "People don't wear veils indoors for no reason. Let us see."

Binta's heart pounded in her chest. She shook her head, gripping the veil even tighter. "No, please, I—"

"It's okay," Detective Moreau said softly, cutting through Caron's pressure. "Miss Binta, you're safe here. We just want to help. You can take off the veil."

Binta looked into Moreau's eyes, seeing the gentleness there but also knowing that this was not a request she could refuse. Slowly, with trembling fingers, she began to loosen the veil. Her mind screamed against it—don't take it off, they'll see, they'll judge—but she had no choice. She let the fabric slip from her face, revealing the long, jagged scar that stretched from her temple, across her cheek, and down to her chin.

There was silence in the room.

The sight of the scar had the impact she feared. Caron's eyes widened slightly, a mix of surprise and something darker flashing across his face. He didn't look away, but Binta could feel the weight of his gaze scrutinising her. Moreau, however, remained calm, her expression unreadable as she took in the disfigurement.

Binta felt a familiar wave of shame rise in her chest, the urge to cover her face overwhelming. She had seen this reaction countless times: the stares, the whispers, the quiet pity, or the open disgust. She shifted uncomfortably, her hands hovering near the veil again, desperate to put it back on.

"How did that happen?" Moreau asked quietly, her voice softer now, not interrogating but curious.

Binta swallowed hard, her voice a whisper. "I got it when I was... younger.

During an attack on my village. It's... it's why I wear the veil."

Moreau's eyes softened even more. She nodded as if understanding the depth of Binta's pain, but she didn't press further. Caron, however, remained cold, his suspicion not fading with the reveal.

"That's quite a scar," he said, his tone hard. "Makes you stand out. We'll need to know where you were last night."

Binta's heart sank. They still thought she was involved in Laurent's murder.

"I was at home," she replied, her voice shaking. "Alone."

"Alone, huh?" Caron said, raising an eyebrow. "Convenient."

Moreau shot him a look, clearly displeased with his approach. "We'll check that out," she said softly, turning back to Binta. "But for now, we just need you to be honest with us. Have you noticed anything strange recently? Anything unusual?"

Binta hesitated. She wanted to tell them about the veil and strange items appearing next to her bed. But how could she? How could she explain the unexplainable without sounding completely insane?

"No," she whispered finally. "Nothing strange."

Moreau sighed, leaning back in her chair. "Alright, Miss Binta. We'll have to follow up, but for now, you can go. Please, don't leave town. We may have more questions."

Binta nodded quickly, her relief palpable. She wrapped her veil back around her face, shielding herself from their gaze once more. But as she left the room, the weight of their suspicion still hung heavy in the air.

And as she stepped out into the cold, wet street, she couldn't shake the feeling that something darker was following her—something she couldn't outrun.

That night, Binta decided not to take off the veil. She had a terrifying nightmare in which a dark entity confronted her and insisted that she take off the veil. The entity showed her what had been happening while she slept. Whenever she took off the mask and slept, the entity possessed her and roamed the streets, taking lives in the name of vengeance. The entity told her that it protected her from those men who tried to harm her and tried to convince her to go with the flow, but Binta refused. The entity became highly violent and choked Binta in her sleep. Binta fought back and woke up breathless.

For the next three days, Binta didn't leave her apartment. She did everything to stay awake. She played loud music, drank cans of energy drinks and nearly drowned herself in coffee. She even taped her eyelids open.

At the break of dawn on the fourth morning, just as she was about to pass out from exhaustion, there was a loud bang on the door. The police had a warrant to search her apartment. She let them in, and while they searched, she slipped out and ran to the roof. The police found a box in her wardrobe containing all the items taken from the murdered men. They chased her to the roof and found her standing on the ledge. As the police coaxed her to step down, the entity yelled at her to jump.

Binta stood on the rooftop, the rain-soaked streets of Paris glistening far below. The police were behind her, their voices a distant murmur, urging her to step away from the ledge. But louder than their words was the voice in her head—the voice of the entity screaming at her to jump off the ledge.

"Jump, Binta!" the entity hissed. "Jump, and you and I will become one forever. You need me. I've protected you from all those men who would have hurt you. I've done what you couldn't do. Jump, and I'll save you again."

The black veil clung to Binta's face, hiding the scar that had defined so much of her life. It was a mask that shielded her from the world but also one that held her prisoner. The entity's voice grew louder, more violent, as the wind whipped around her. "They'll never stop! They'll always look at you like you're a monster. I can make sure they never hurt you again. Jump, Binta!"

Trembling, Binta closed her eyes, but instead of darkness, she saw the vast

Mambilla Plateau—the land she had left behind so long ago. She imagined herself as the Marsh Harrier, soaring above the hills, the wind beneath her wings. She remembered her mother's stories, the beauty of the bird that always returned home. It wasn't a prey. It feared nothing. It was free.

With her eyes closed and her mind soaring high over the Mambilla Plateau, she had a moment of clarity.

The veil embodied the darkness she harbours within—the unresolved pain, anger, and fear. It guarded her from the outside world, but it also kept her locked within her trauma. It shielded her from immediate harm but also trapped her in a cycle of violence and self-denial. By hiding her face, the veil reinforces the idea that she must reject her true self in order to feel safe. It unlocks her subconscious rage and trauma, allowing a darker, more violent version of herself to emerge. The veil is like a doorway between her waking, conscious self—who craves peace and healing—and the broken, vengeful part of her that is still stuck in the moment of her family's massacre, molested in the IDP camp and ridiculed in Paris. It offered the illusion of control and safety but, in truth, amplified her internal turmoil. By accepting it, she protected and betrayed herself, surrendering to an easy solution rather than facing the difficult journey of self-acceptance and healing. The veil gives her what she thinks she wants—protection from the world—but at the cost of her soul, as it nurtures her darkest impulses. In that moment of lucidity, she realised the true cost of wearing the veil.

    The entity went off on a tirade. "Death is the only escape from pain. Your scars are too deep to heal. Jump, and you will find peace, an end to the suffering, nightmares, and hiding. They will never see you for anything but your scars. Jump, and you will be reunited with your family."

The entity continued to scream, but Binta's heart was elsewhere. She could see beyond the lies. She knew the entity was the culmination of her despair, anger, and a deep desire for escape. It was her internal struggle between life and death, between healing and self-destruction, personified in the figure of her demon. She rejected the entity's command and chose healing over destruction, vulnerability over hiding, and, ultimately, life over death.

Slowly, she reached up and touched the veil that had become a symbol of her torment. She hesitated momentarily, then pulled it off in an act of defiance. The rain stung her bare skin, the cold air biting at her scarred face, but she felt no shame.

With a steady hand, Binta tossed the veil into the air, watching as it fluttered away, carried by the wind. She stepped back from the ledge, not toward the void, but toward life.

Detective Moreau, watching her closely, rushed forward and caught Binta in her arms. She held her tightly, whispering, "It's okay. You're safe now."

Binta leaned into the embrace, letting tears come not from fear but from relief. She had fought the darkness within her and won.

In the following months, Binta was sent to a medical institution, where she received the care she had long needed. It was a place of healing, not punishment, and for the first time in years, she allowed herself to face her trauma head-on. She underwent intensive therapy, and with each session, she began to reclaim parts of herself that had been lost in her years of suffering.

She no longer hid her face. The scarfs, once her constant companions, lay folded in a drawer. The scar that had once made her feel so monstrous became a part of her identity but no longer something that defined her. It was a mark of survival, not shame.

When she was finally discharged, Binta had a new sense of purpose. Inspired by Louise's kindness and her own experiences, she decided to join a humanitarian organisation. She felt called to help those who had endured the same kind of pain and trauma she had.

Months later, Binta stood again in northeastern Nigeria, the air dry and warm, the Sahel stretching out before her. This time, she had returned as an aid worker, ready to help others displaced by conflict and violence, just as Louise had done for her.

As she stepped into the refugee camp, the memories of her past swirled around her—the loss, the fear, the pain. But instead of being weighed down by them, she felt lighter. She had transformed her suffering into strength.

With her head held high and her scar uncovered for all to see, Binta smiled softly, knowing she had found her way back to herself. No longer hiding, no longer running—she had become the Marsh Harrier she had always dreamed of being, soaring above her past and returning home stronger than ever.

- Other titles by Kele Chi -

DREAM QUEST

HOLIDAY HOUSE

Printed in Great Britain
by Amazon